This book is dedicated to my lovely Granny Pam, who inspired me into writing this book!

To val & Derek

Hope you
enjoy the book

love

Hannah

Chapter 1

On a summer's day Melissa was walking up Bakers Street on her way to college. She had her earphones in and was singing as she was walking. At the same Melissa's best friends Jake, Aiden and Oliver were walking on the opposite side of the road chatting to each other. When they saw Melissa walking past Bakers Street, their faces lit up.

"Look guys there's Melissa", Jake announced.

"Oh yeah, let's go and walk with her", Aiden replied.

The three boys walked across the road and walked up behind Melissa. Aiden went up behind her and put his hands over her eyes.

"Guess who?"

Melissa stopped walking and turned around to see who it was. She realized it was the boys and took her ear phones out.

"Hi guys are you ok?" she asked.

"Yeah we are ok", Aiden replied.

"We saw you walking on the other side of the road and thought we would surprise you", Jake added.

"It's only three more days until London", Oliver stated.

"I know, it's going to be great", Melissa replied.

"I can't wait until we go to Madame Tussuards and see all the wax figures!" Aiden exclaimed.

"Me too", Jake responded.

The four friends continued walking up to the college entrance. There was the usual crowd, and what a surprise, it was the two love-birds, Ella and Ben.

"GET A ROOM!" The four friends shouted in unison.

"SHUT UP!!" The two love-birds shouted back.

"Can the guys and I sit by you in class Mellissa?" Jake asked.

"Yeah course you can", Melissa replied.

"I'm going to love London, it will be so romantic", Ella said whilst looking at Ben gazing into his eyes as they nose kiss.

"Uugh!" The four friends groaned in disgust.

"While you two love-birds are having your moments, the boys and I will be off exploring the sites. Right guys?" Melissa said

Aiden agreed. "Yeah I would rather hang out with my mates than spend a day with them two".

All the teenagers went into their form classes to get their marks. When the bell went for first period the teenagers waited for each other outside their form classes and walked to English.

They all sat in pairs. Melissa sat next to Aiden and Jake sat next to Oliver directly in front of them. Melissa was having a hard time doing her work because she couldn't stop thinking about the trip to London.

"I can't concentrate on my work today, I've got London, London, London in my head", Melissa said whilst putting her hand on her forehead.

"Dead right", Aiden agreed.

Jake and Oliver had finished their first piece of work and turned around to talk to Aiden and Melissa.

"Melissa did you know it's Aiden's birthday tomorrow?" Jake questioned.

"Oh crap. I'm sorry Aiden, I completely forgot", Melissa said whlist throwing her pen in frustration.

"That's ok. Do you want to come with us tomorrow night? We are only going bowling".

"I would love to".

"Ok I will get my Mum to pick you up at half six".

"Who else is going?"

"It's just us lot".

"Aww good. I just hope Ben and Ella don't go off like last time".

"Me too".

Chapter 2

The following day soon came around. Everyone was at The White House bowling alley for Aiden's birthday party. Melissa gave Aiden a card and a watch.

"Happy Birthday Aiden", Melissa announced.

"Thank you Mel", Aiden replied whlist giving his best friend a hug.

"I've got a little prezzie for you", Mellissa said whlist giving the present to Aiden.

"Thanks Melissa that's very kind of you", Aiden replied.

Aiden's face said it all as he opened the present.

"Aww thanks Mel, you shouldn't have", Aiden said whilst giving his best friend another hug.

"You're welcome", Melissa replied.

"What have you got mate?" Jake asked.

"A lovely card and an amazing watch", Aiden responded.

"That's nice of you Mel", Jake said.

"Thanks again Melissa, you're the best", Aiden said.

"You are more than welcome", Melissa replied.

"A little bit of flirting going on here Aiden", Jake said.

"Shut up Jake Melissa and I are just friends, nothing else. Aren't we Mel?" Aiden responded annoyed.

"Yeah we are just friends, so keep your nose out", Melissa added annoyed as well.

"Ok calm down, don't get your knickers in a twist", Jake responded.

Everyone got into two teams and played two rounds of bowling, the boys were dead competitive and kept doing pranks on each other to make them lose points, however the girls were dead competitive as well. They had won the first game and the boys won the second game, and everyone was having a great time.

Three hours later the party was over. Everyone went home to get some sleep as they had to get up early for their trip to London.

Chapter 3

The next day everyone was up bright and early ready to go. Melissa came through the security section ad walked into the waiting area for the trains to arrive. Her face lit up when she saw Aiden sitting on the bench.

"Hi early bird, how long have you been here for?" Melissa asked as she gave Aiden a hug.

"About 5 minutes... been up since five o'clock this morning. I've been checking these bloody train tickets a hundred times", Aiden replied frustrated.

"We are only going to London Aiden, not emigrating".

Fifteen minutes later Jake and Oliver arrived in the waiting area with their two suitcases.

"Hi guys, are you both excited for the trip?" Melissa asked giving them both a hug.

"Yeah I can't wait", Jake replied.

"Me either", Oliver added.

"Have you packed everything you need?" Aiden asked.

"I think I packed everything I own", Oliver replied.

Jake looked towards the waiting area doors to see Ella and Ben walking in holding hands with their two suitcases and two backpacks.

"Are those college books you have got there?" Jake asked whlist looking inside the bag.

"Just a few for the train", Ben replied.

"You must be joking", Aiden scoffed.

"This is a holiday guys, college has been left behind", Melissa added.

"We know that, but Ben and I want to study our French", Ella responded.

Melissa and Aiden just looked at each other and raised their eyebrows.

"Why do you think you will need to speak French in London?" Oliver questioned.

"Very funny smarty pants, what is the most common language spoken in London?" Ben replied.

"I do know there are over 250 languages spoken in London. How's that for knowledge?" Oliver responded giving Ben a smirk.

"Ok Google", Aiden said smiling.

"Ok that's enough college work, it's fun time", Melissa said.

"Where are those girls? The train will be here in ten minutes", Aiden complained.

"I will ring Sophie and find out where they are", Melissa said whilst getting her phone out of her pocket.

Melissa walked over to the other side of the platform and phoned Sophie.

"Hello?"

"WHERE THE HELL ARE YOU? The train leaves in ten minutes and Aiden is getting stressed out", Melissa shouted.

"Calm down Mel, we are just walking over the bridge now", Sophie replied calmly.

"Well get a bloody move on then", Melissa responded.

Melissa hung up the phone and just as she put her phone in her pocket, all the girls turned up with loads of suitcases. Melissa walked back to the boys to mess the girls with their suitcases.

"No wonder you're last minute, you have more luggage than any of us", Oliver said sarcastically.

"The train is coming guys", Aiden called.

"ALL ABOARD!" Melissa shouted.

Aiden passed everyone their tickets as they boarded the train- he had reserved seats for everyone to be together.

"Seats 72-92, coach 3 guys, let's move", Aiden ordered.

Some of the friends were sat down in their seats getting out their devices, eating food, etc. And some were just putting their suitcases on the trays above the seats.

"I will put your suitcase on the tray for you Melissa", Aiden said whilst picking up the suitcase.

"Are you sure Aiden?" Melissa asked.

"Yeah I'm sure, you sit down and relax", Aiden replied.

Ben and Jake were watching this flirting going on; Ben elbowed Jake when he saw Aiden helping Melissa.

"Look at Aiden putting Melissa's suitcase away", Ben whispered to Jake.

"Yeah what a gentleman", Jake said.

It seemed ages for everyone to get all the suitcases inside the storage trays because they put loads of stuff inside it. There was a hell of a racket with everyone talking at once on the train.

"These city trains are great; we have each got a table. Who's bought poker cards?" Oliver said.

"I'm so excited, this is my first I have been on a trip on my own", Millie said.

"On your own, there are nineteen of us with you", Paige replied.

"Oh you know what I mean", Millie responded.

"I wonder what the hotel is going to be like", Tilly said.

"Mum says all Premier Inn hotels are the same", Darcy stated.

"Goodnight's sleep or your money back", Oliver said laughing.

"Well I bet we all get our money back, I can't imagine we will sleep that well!" Lottie exclaimed.

"Well not tonight", Brooke responded.

"Speak for yourself, after this journey and what time I was up this morning I will sleep like a log", Jake said whilst yawning.

"News for you mate, have you heard Ben snore?" Oliver responded.

"Are you having a laugh? Does he BLOODY snore?" Jake replied angrily.

"Language!!" Melissa exclaimed.

"Well if he does he can swap and go in the girl's room".

Chapter 4

A few hours later the train was pulling up into Euston and everyone was getting even more excited. As soon as the train stopped, everyone started getting their suitcases out of the trays.

"I've got your suitcase Mel", Aiden said whilst getting it down.

"Aww thanks Aiden you are too kind", Melissa replied following Aiden to the exit.

"I best go and help Darcy and Olivia. Have you seen how MUCH they have got?" Oliver said whilst looking at the girls.

"Are you feeling alright Oliver?" Jake said smirking.

"GET LOST!" Oliver replied angrily.

Everyone got off the train and headed towards the notice board to get directions to the hotel. Oliver just looked at the food places because he was hungry.

"First stop for us all is KFC", Oliver said.

"Me and Sophie will go to McDonalds", Darcy said.

"According to the plan, KFC is five minutes that way, follow me guys", Jake ordered.

All the friends followed Jake to where KFC was. They all went inside and sat down by the window. Aiden was asking them what they wanted to eat, and Melissa was writing the orders down on a piece of paper.

"Can we not get so many buckets between us all?" Oliver suggested.

"Not a good idea with what you eat", Jake said sarcastically.

"Jake do me a favour and collect all the money for the food and help me carry the food back instead of making sarcastic comments", Aiden said angrily.

Everyone had to work out what they had to give Jake. They didn't have to wait long before Aiden and Jake were back with the food and the drinks. Aiden dished out the food orders for everyone that Melissa had written down. They all tucked in and thanked Aiden and Jake for organising it. It seemed ages since they had breakfast even though they had a packed lunch on the train.

"That was great, anybody leaving any of theirs?" Oliver said whilst wiping his face with a napkin.

"You can have these fries if you like", Lottie offered.

"You can have this chicken leg as well", Brooke added.

"Any more?" Oliver asked being greedy.

"I told you he's like a human dustbin", Jake said.

After Oliver had eaten all of the leftovers, they left the restaurant and met up with Darcy and Sophie outside McDonalds.

"I bet you would have liked a nice chicken leg Darcy", Oliver said in amusement.

"Don't be tight Oliver, you know she's a vegetarian", Melissa responded sarcastically.

"And I'm a Capricorn", Oliver replied smirking at Darcy.

"Very funny…NOT!" I've heard every vegetarian joke thank you very much", Darcy said in an annoyed tone.

"You are making me feel guilty now Darcy", Sophie said.

"Well, I know when I see a little lamb in the field I cannot think of eating it", Darcy replied sarcastically.

"Neither can I, that's why I only eat BIG steaks", Oliver responded.

"ENOUGH!!" Aiden shouted.

"Right guys I think it's about time we start heading towards the taxi ranks", Melissa said.

Everyone followed Melissa and started walking. They got in in a black cab and told the taxi driver to take them to the Premier Inn. It took ten minutes to get there. They all got out of the taxi and went into the hotel. Booking in was mad, there was a huge queue. Melissa had the booking reservations ready for the receptionist.

"The lady at the desk will give each of you a key and a room a number", Melissa said.

"A key?" Brooke questioned.

"Ok swipe card", Melissa responded.

When they got to the reception desk the lady gave each of them a swipe card and a room number. Melissa, Ella, Olivia, Sophie, and Darcy were in one room, the rest of the girls in another room, and the boys in a room.

"Are you alright on the first floor Mel?" Ella asked.

"Yeah I'm alright with that, it's just escalators I don't like", Melissa responded.

"I will bring your suitcase up Mel", Aiden said.

"Thanks Aiden", Melissa replied.

The girls went upstairs in the lift whilst the boys took the stairs.

"Is that so you can get to know her room number?" Jake said smirking.

"Get lost Jake", Aiden replied angrily.

The three boys eventually got in their room except Oliver who was still helping the girls with their suitcases.

"Gives me time to have a sleep and test these beds out… otherwise it's a money back guarantee", Oliver said.

"Who are you Lenny Henry?" Brooke responded.

"Who has got the short straw having to share a room with you?" Lottie said.

"Talking about Lenny Henry, did everyone see Comic Relief?" Tilly asked.

"I missed it", Millie responded.

"How?" Paige asked.

"I forgot it was on", Millie replied.

"Forgot?" Oliver responded.

"Yes, but I did hear they raised seventy-five million pounds", Millie said.

"Oh, it was so sad at times", Lottie said.

"Let's just forget about it", Tilly responded.

"Come on rooms", Brooke ordered.

In the girl's room Melissa, Ella, Olivia, Sophie and Darcy were all lying on the bed when Aiden came in with Melissa's suitcase. Melissa got up and went to give him a hug.

"Thank you Aiden, you didn't have to do that", Melissa said.

"Well I'm happy to help my friends ou, I will let you girls get changed and will see you later", Aiden replied.

"See ya, and thanks again", Melissa responded.

"My pleasure", Aiden said smiling.

"Shut the door behind you", Sophie said whilst laughing.

"Shut up!" Aiden responded smirking.

All the girls started to unpack their things. Meanwhile in the boy's room, Jake was jumping on the bed, Aiden and Ben were unpacking their things, and Oliver was having a shower.

"This is great boys you should try it", Jake said whilst jumping up and down.

"Will you stop acting like a child Jake, get down from the bed", Aiden said firmly.

"What time are we meeting the girls then?" Oliver said as he walked out of the shower.

"They are just unpacking, I will text Melissa and find out", Aiden replied.

"Aiden has just texted me to see what time we will meet them", Melissa said to her friends.

"Well what time does Charlie and the Chocolate Factory start?" Ella asked.

"I've got all the theatre times in my diary", Olivia replied.

"Organized… I'm impressed", Sophie responded.

"It starts at seven-thirty", Olivia said.

"So we will need to eat first", Melissa said.

"I'm starving", Sophie responded.

"That's because you ate rabbit food", Ella said.

"I only went with Darcy so she wasn't on her own", Sophie replied.

"Ok guys what time?" Melissa asked.

"Six o'clock", Olivia replied.

"Ok so that gives us time to find a place to eat and then we can get taxis to the restaurant and the Apollo Theatre which is near Convent Gardens", Melissa said.

Melissa texted Aiden.

"Yes... we will meet at six o'clock", Aiden says reading the message out.

"Did she put any kisses?" Jake responded smirking.

"Shut up Jake we are best mates, and yes she did put a kiss", Aiden said annoyed.

Chapter 5

Back in the girls room they were all getting ready to go out.

"It's half five... we all need to get a move on", Darcy ordered.

"Melissa's all ready to go", Sophie said.

"Yeah all dolled up for anyone special" Olivia questioned.

"Yes Aiden", Darcy joked.

Melissa turned around from doing make-up as soon as she heard Aiden's name.

"WHAT! We are just good mates that's all, he makes me laugh and he's kind", Melissa said in a temper.

"Ok keep your knickers on", Ella responded.

"Oh, you are getting all dolled up for your BELOVED BEN", Melissa replied.

"Jealous, are you?" Ella questioned.

"You MUST be joking. He's not my type.... Checked it on the love calculator", Melissa scoffed.

"You get on with him well enough", Ella responded.

"Yeah he's a mate.. one of the boys. Why wouldn't I get on with him?" Melissa replied.

"Well you would rather go out with Aiden than Ben", Ella said.

"Ella, we have been over this a million time, AIDEN IS JUST A MATE NOTHING ELSE ALRIGHT!!!" Melissa shouted.

"Right guys are we all ready to go?" Olivia said awkwardly.

All the girls headed downstairs to the foyer where the boys and the rest of the girls were waiting. They were all looking smart in their casual clothes.

"Do we know where we are going to eat?" Aiden questioned.

"Anywhere where there is food", Oliver responded.

"Typical", Aiden replied whlist rolling his eyes.

"We quite fancy Chinese, how does that sound?" Olivia suggested.

"Great", Aiden replied.

"Well Darcy can join us at Chinese, there are plenty of vegetarian dishes that she can choose from", Sophie said.

"I will go and ask that dishy receptionist where best to go", Oliver said.

"You would", Jake replied.

The receptionist told Oliver there was a really nice Chinese restaurant called Water Margin about two streets away and gave him directions to turn right outside the hotel, and that it was on the next corner. Oliver thanked her and returned back to tell the others.

"Follow me guys, she said this place does the best FEAST you could possibly get for under a tenner", Oliver said.

"Sounds good to me", Jake responded.

They started walking to the restaurant. The receptionist had given Oliver a leaflet to look at all the different foods and prices that they had on the menu.

"Ten pounds for vegetables", Darcy moaned.

"Your fault for being vegetarian", Oliver responded.

"I'm sure you could get just a vegetarian dish cheaper, it's Oliver who likes the sound of a feast", Melissa said laughing.

"I bet you like the sound of a feast Mel with what you eat", Ben commented.

"I just eat meals NOT rubbish like you eat every five minutes", Melissa responded.

They arrived at the restaurant and it looked really smart from the outside. They went inside the restaurant and it looked even better.

"This looks posh", Lottie commented.

"We are in London Lottie, not Rhyl", Aiden said.

"Hey what's wrong with Rhyl?" Lottie replied.

"I meant there are thousands of restaurants here, they all have to look and be good, it's competition", Aiden responded.

They were all approached by a Chinese man called Mr Wong. He showed them to a large table and there was enough chairs for all the friends to sit down. It was at the back of the restaurant.

He was very chatty asking Darcy where they were all from, however Oliver was hungry.

"Can't we just have the bloody menu?" Oliver whispered to Aiden.

"Yeah I'm sick of him telling us about his life story", Aiden whispered back to Oliver.

"Hey, I will interrupt them", Melissa whispered to the boys.

"Go on Mel you do it", Aiden whispered back.

"Excuse me, please could we have the menu?" Melissa asked the waiter.

"Certainly", the waiter replied whilst handing out the menus.

"Thank god for that", Oliver said whilst looking at the menu.

Everyone selected what they wanted to eat from the menu.

"Oliver, are you having chips as well as rice?" Melissa questioned.

"Yeah I told you I'm starving", Oliver replied.

"Nothing new then", Jake commented.

Mr Wong delivered a huge bowl of Prawn crackers for the teenagers to share, prior to bringing out the main meals. Everyone enjoyed their meals except Darcy.

"I didn't like mine", Darcy complained.

"You always moan and complain Darcy. What didn't you like this time?" Aiden said.

"I don't ALWAYS moan and complain!" Darcy responded angrily.

"Yes you do Darcy, if it's not been food it's when you don't get your own way", Melissa added.

"You're just agreeing with Aiden", Darcy replied angrily.

"Yes, just stop moaning", Melisa responded.

Everyone paid their £10 to Darcy who was collecting the money.

"She wants to look good in front of Mr Wong", Olivia said.

"Who's going to order a taxi then?" Melissa asked.

"We are in London Melissa, the big city; we just go outside and flag a black cab", Jake said.

"Jake do you have to be so awkward at times?" Aiden responded annoyed.

They all jumped in a taxi to the theatre.

"How easy was that to get a taxi, this is great no messing waiting", Melissa said.

"Bet it's not three quid like Leddans?" Oliver responded.

"What are you on about?" Melissa questioned.

"What funny man means there is the Leddans taxi firm at home only charge three quid for anywhere in Rhyl. You obviously don't use taxis often either, or you don't pay", Aiden explained whilst pointing at Oliver.

"Oh I get it now", Melissa replied.

The taxi arrived at the Apollo Theatre. They went inside and it was massive compared to the Rhyl Pavilion Theatre. It had posh carpets and old wallpaper. They approached the Charlie and the Chocolate Factory seating, and it appeared there was going to be a long wait.

"There is such a long queue", Lottie said.

"It moves fast though, it was like this when I went to see Mamma Mia last year", Melissa stated.

The queue finally moved a lot faster. They each got a ticket and were pleased they could all sit together.

"I think we were lucky guys getting so many seats together", Melissa said.

"You're right there Melissa, perhaps we should book for the other shows we are planning to see", Tilly responded.

"You have just got yourself the job Tilly", Aiden said.

"Where is Oliver?" Tilly questioned.

"He's gone to the Kiosk", Jake replied.

"He's such a greedy pig, he has just eaten half of the Chinese", Melissa responded.

"Here he comes now", Jake said.

"Are those for sharing?" Aiden asked.

"No way, get your own", Oliver responded.

"How can you eat chocolate and sweets? I'm stuffed after the Chinese", Ben questioned.

"Easy", Oliver replied.

Everyone was all settled in their seats enjoying their refreshments, when all of a sudden the music came on. The girls jumped out of their skin. It was a brilliant first half, everyone enjoyed it. Ben and Ella kept nose kissing and holding hands the whole way through it.

"ICE CREAM TIME!!" Oliver shouted.

Olivia, Oliver, and Darcy all went to get the ice creams.

"Aiden did you see what Ben and Ella were doing throughout the performance?" Melissa asked.

"What were they doing?" Aiden replied.

"They were nose kissing and holding hands", Melissa said.

"How romantic…. NOT!" Aiden responded.

Oliver, Olivia, and Darcy all came back with the ice creams. The group enjoyed every single bit of it. Fifteen minutes later the music came back on for the second half.

The second half seemed longer than the first half but there was a range of good acting and good screening. All the teenagers walked out of the screening booth and headed towards the exit of the theatre.

"My favourite character was Veronica because it reminds of Darcy", Tilly said.

"How does that remind you of Darcy?" Brooke asked.

"Moody", Tilly replied.

"Oh I thought you meant a pain in the foot", Oliver joked.

"Hey stop picking on me", Darcy said feeling upset.

"We are only joking, you know that", Lottie said.

"Yeah it will probably be my turn to be the butt of the wisecracks tomorrow", Jake responded.

"No mate you are a joke everyday", Aiden said jokingly.

Everyone started laughing in a fun way and walked outside the theatre to look for a taxi. They hailed one across the road from the theatre, jumped in, and told the taxi driver to take them back to their hotel. Ten minutes later they arrived at the hotel, and were left wondering what to do.

"What shall we do now?" Sophie asked.

"We can go for a drink in the lounge", Melissa suggested.

"Sounds good to me, let's go there then", Aiden said.

They were about to head towards the bar when they bumped into Melissa's support workers, Mrs Courtney Hudges, and Mrs Demi Wright.

"Hi Melissa fancy seeing you here", Mrs Hudges stated.

"Hi Mrs Hudges, Mrs Wright, how are you?" Melissa replied.

"We are good thanks", Mrs Wright responded.

"Can I get you a drink ladies?" Aiden asked.

"That would be lovely", Mrs Hudges replied.

"What do you drink?" Aiden asked.

"White wine please Aiden", Mrs Wright replied.

"Coming right up", Aiden said walking up to the bar.

Just then the rest of the teachers from college were coming out of the bathroom.

"I best go and get some more drinks", Jake said.

"It's white wine all round Jake please", Mrs Hudges said.

"Let's go and see if we can find a table big enough for us all", Melissa said.

"I will go and see if there is room", Oliver offered.

Oliver went to find a seat for them all to sit down whilst Aiden and Jake returned with the drinks.

"You would make a good waiter Aiden", Mrs Wright commented.

"You can give me the tips", Jake joked.

"Follow me guys", Oliver said on approach while returning to find a table.

Everyone followed Oliver to where he found some seats.

"Well done Oliver, this is great", Melissa said.

"So what have you guys been up to then?" Mrs Hudges asked.

"Well for starters, poor Melissa was terrified of the escalators so I had to hold her hand. None of the boys offered to help. They just stood there like nothing was going on. I didn't mind doing it because she is my best friend", Aiden explained.

"You would like to be more than just friends wouldn't you Aiden?" Jake said whilst smirking.

"Shut up Jake, Melissa and I are just friends I DO NOT FANCY HER. No offence Melissa", Aiden said.

"Oh, it's alright Aiden", Melissa responded with a sigh.

"I mean I do like her... she's kind, funny, and great looking", Aiden commented.

"Fair enough, I said the same thing about you", Melissa responded.

"Really?" Aiden questioned.

"Yeah, you're my best friend Aiden- you're kind, you're funny, and you are very helpful, plus your extra good looking", Melissa said smiling.

"Aww thanks Mel", Aiden replied smiling.

"Sorry to interrupt your romance but why don't you ask Melissa out already?" Jake said.

"Me and Melissa are happy being friends aren't we Mel?" Aiden said.

"Yeah best friends forever", Melissa replied.

"More drinks anyone?" Lottie questioned.

"Yes please Lottie, beers for me and the lads, and make it two for Aiden because he needs some courage to make a move on Melissa", Oliver responded.

"Cut it Oliver, I've already said Melissa and I are just happy being best friends, so stop going on about it ok", Aiden said annoyed.

"Alright calm down, take a chill pill", Oliver responded.

"What would you like to drink ladies?" Darcy asked.

"No more for me thank you Darcy, I'm tired", Mrs Hudges.

"Me too. Let's go Mrs Hudges. We will see you tomorrow guys", Mrs Wright said.

Mrs Hudges and Mrs Wright headed towards the door at the same time and both ended up bumping into it.

"What are we doing tomorrow?" Olivia asked.

"Madame Tussauds, the plan is to go after breakfast no messing about", Melissa ordered.

"Early birds are we then?" Olivia asked.

"Yeah otherwise it will be lunchtime before we get anywhere", Aiden replied.

"Goodnight guys", Melissa said.

Everyone went into their rooms and went to sleep. The following morning the group all met in the dining hall for breakfast.

Chapter 6

"Full English everyone?" Oliver questioned.

"Typical Oliver and food", Melissa joked.

Everyone went to get something to eat as it was a help yourself buffet. They all enjoyed their breakfast and went into the foyer.

"Ok is everyone ready to go?" Aiden asked.

"Hang on I need to go and get some cash", Ben said.

"I wish Ben would get bloody organized", Jake complained.

"Oh I think I will just go upstairs and get a jacket just in case", Olivia said.

"In case of what?" Lottie questioned.

"Oh shut up", Olivia responded.

Once Ben and Olivia came downstairs all the teenagers headed towards the bus stop which was 200 yards from the hotel. They arrived at the bus stop just as the bus pulled up, and everyone purchased an all-day ticket as the plan was to do the London Bus Tour.

"Are you ok upstairs Mel?" Aiden asked.

"Yeah. I don't mind where we sit", Melissa replied.

"How many stops to Madame Tussauds please?" Oliver asked the conductor.

"It takes 10 minutes to get there….. I will give you a shout", the conductor said.

They all went upstairs to see the sites of London. Ten minutes later the conductor shouted that the next stop was Madame Tussauds. All the teenagers headed downstairs ready to get off. They all got off the bus and walked to the entrance.

"Look at that queue", Tilly pointed out.

"It will soon go down", Lottie responded.

"There are THREE ticket booths!" Darcy exclaimed.

"I wish the queue would bloody go faster, I can't wait to see the Little Mix wax figures", Millie said excitedly.

"You would", Melissa said.

"Shut up Melissa", Millie shouted.

"Hey don't tell Melissa to shut up, at least she's excited to see ALL the wax figures, you just want to see Little Mix", Lottie said.

"Come on guys let's not bicker, we've got loads of exciting things to see", Darcy said.

They finally got to a ticket booth, and as soon as they entered the room Melissa saw her favourite comedian and actor Jack Whitehall.

"Oh my god! It's Jack Whitehall I love him, he's my idol!" Melissa exclaimed.

"Aiden looks jealous. Are you ok Aiden?" Jake said whilst smiling.

"No I'm not jealous of a wax figure", Aiden responded.

Melissa was taking photographs of the girls with Jack Whitehall. Then she passed the camera to Aiden.

"Please can you take a photograph of me with Jack Whitehall!" Melissa asked Aiden.

"Ok anything for you", Aiden replied.

"WIT WHOO", the boys said in unison.

"Cut it out", Aiden said annoyed.

"We are going to have to drag Melissa away from this guy", Tilly said to Lottie.

"We sure are. Come on Mel", Lottie said whilst grabbing Melissa's hand.

"I'm looking for Jamie Redknapp", Jake said.

"Paige can you come with me to see Little Mix?" Millie asked.

"Looks like we are just looking for our idols", Oliver said.

"Hey look- Miley Cyrus", Lottie said whilst pointing at the wax figure.

"Looks nothing like her", Oliver responded.

All of a sudden Tilly screams her heart out as she saw One Direction wax figures.

"Aiden could you take a photograph of me with One Direction?" Tilly asked.

"No", Aiden replied.

"Well you did it for Melissa", Tilly responded.

"Yeah well she's my best friend", Aiden said.

"Why can't you do it for me then?" Tilly questioned.

"You are just a friend", Aiden said.

"I will give you a sloppy kiss if you don't", Tilly flirted.

"I will take it for a sloppy kiss!" Oliver flirted back.

"Yeah No! Lottie take one of me", Tilly said.

"Next stop dungeons", Jake said.

They all headed to the dungeons in fear.

"Oh my god. I'm too scared to go in there", Ella said.

"Me too", Melissa said,

"Here hold our hands", Aiden, Ben , and Jake said in unison.

They went into the dungeons holding hands scared and nervous of the unknown. There was a figure dressed as a nun coming towards them with an axe in each hand. All of a sudden a coffin lid opened in front of them and Oliver jumped out of it.

"Stop fooling around Oliver, it's not only the poor girls you scared to death", Aiden said annoyed.

They all exited the dungeons shaking to death. Aiden and Melissa realized that they were still holding hands and quickly pulled away. They all went to the gift shop to buy their professional photos they had with different celebrity wax figures and merchandises for themselves and family. Aiden put his hand out for a taxi and they all headed straight back to the hotel to get ready for the Night Bus Tour.

Chapter 7

"You are making a special effort tonight Aiden", Jake said.

"WHAT!" Aiden shouted as he turned around to face the boys.

"We all know you fancy Melissa", Jake said.

Aiden went as red as a tomato and looked down to the floor. Meanwhile in the girl's room they were all getting ready to go out and talking about Melissa's romance with Aiden.

"Melissa is dolled up ready to impress ... any guesses who that could be for anyone?" Olivia said.

"You do look nice Melissa seriously", Ella commented.

"Aiden will love that outfit", Darcy added.

"We all love it- you have some really cool clothes Melissa", Sophie commented.

"Thanks Sophie-down to mum's influence", Melissa replied.

"So who do you want to impress?" Ella questioned.

"What do you mean?" Melissa replied.

"We all know you fancy Aiden", Darcy said.

Melissa went bright red and tried hard not to smile.

"Admit it Mel", Olivia said.

"Ok… I'll tell you, but DON'T tell the boys, especially Aiden and Jake", Melissa replied.

"We promise we won't tell the boys", Sophie responded.

"Ok... I do have a crush on Aiden", Melissa said smiling.

"WIT WHOO!" The girls said in unison.

"Melissa's in love", Olivia sang.

"Bloody hell! Is that the time already, come on girls let's go", Melissa said looking at her watch.

All the girls went downstairs and the boys were already in reception. Melissa and Aiden just kept smiling at each other. Aiden went bright red and turned to Jake.

"Why have you gone bright red mate?" Jake questioned.

"Because I'm nervous", Aiden replied.

"Nervous of what?" Jake questioned.

"I'm nervous of talking to Melissa", Aiden replied.

"You were confident before with her", Jake responded.

"I know, but this is different I'm going make the first move tonight", Aiden said.

Melissa was talking to the girls on the other side of the foyer.

"Aiden looks very handsome tonight", Melissa commented.

"Are you going to be extra friendly then tonight Mel?" Darcy questioned.

"Very funny", Melissa replied in a sarcastic tone.

Melissa and the girls walked over to see the boys.

"I like what you are wearing tonight Aiden, where did you get your shirt from?" Melissa asked.

"Chester", Aiden responded going bright red.

"Oh, I didn't mean to embarrass you, I really mean it you look really nice", Melissa replied.

"Oh, thanks Melissa, you look stunning yourself. It really suits you with your hair up like that", Aiden commented.

"Ella did it for me- she is so rough it killed me", Melissa replied laughing.

"Ok guys are we ready to go, the bus is due in five minutes?" Oliver asked his friends.

They all headed towards the bus stop and just as they reached it the bus arrived. All the teenagers walked on the bus and headed up the stairs.

"I'm going near the front Aiden", Melissa called to Aiden.

Aiden made his way behind Oliver, pushing him out of the way making Jake trip up the stairs hurting his knee and elbow. They were all trying to get the seat by Melissa.

Melissa turned around and saw all the pushing and shoving the boys were making.

"RIGHT GUYS! STOP MESSING ABOUT, I know I'm gorgeous but you don't have to fight over me! Aiden sit there by me", Melissa shouted.

"See, I'm her favourite", Aiden commented to the boys.

"Just because you fancy her, and want to ask her out", Jake responded.

All the lads sat down by the girls, and Aiden sat by Melissa.

Aiden casually puts his arm around Melissa making the first move. Melissa looked to see Aiden's arm on her shoulder and felt a bit upset and uncomfortable because she wanted to make the first move. She turned to Aiden and raised her eyebrows.

"What are you doing?" Melissa questioned.

"You had a creepy crawler on your shoulder", Aiden replied whilst moving his arm away from Melissa feeling embarrassed.

Oliver decided to move over behind Aiden and Melissa and tease both of them.

"The only creepy crawler is you" Oliver said jokingly.

"What an excuse", Lottie remarked listening to the conversation.

Melissa started to laugh and smiled at Aiden.

"Has the creepy crawler gone yet?" Oliver joked whilst leaning back in his seat.

"Very funny", Aiden responded.

"What is going on, what have I missed?" Jake said as he was standing up.

"You've not missed nothing mate, just enjoy the ride", Aiden replied.

The night bus tour was really good. Everything lit up in the streets and on the bus as well, and all the buildings and shops were impressive.

"I wish we could get off here, I really fancy jumping into the fountain", Oliver said.

"Oh yeah and get locked up. DIV!" Melissa said annoyed.

"They don't lock that up on New Year's Eve", Oliver replied.

"Could that be because there are too many of them?" Lottie questioned.

They were all approaching the Houses of Parliament and Big Ben... the buildings looked absolutely amazing when they all lit up with bright colours.

"Aren't we supposed to be conserving electricity- what must their bill be? My Mum screams her head off if we leave a light on in a room we have just left", Jake said.

"Mine too", Darcy added.

"It is money well spent; London brings in so many tourists that is good for the country and economy", Aiden said.

"Politician now Mr Perry are we?" Oliver said jokingly.

"You are just the joker of the group that's for sure", Melissa said smiling.

The group finally got off the bus for a break and walked to the nearest pub that they could find. They came across one which looked like a dump, went in and it was so packed, all the friends didn't know where to sit or what to do.

"Where do you guys want to go?" Ella asked her friends.

"Don't worry I will find a comfy place where we can all sit down and relax", Oliver said.

"Oliver is brilliant; he is always the one finding us a decent seat", Melissa commented.

All the teenagers followed Oliver, and as usual he found them comfy seats at the back of the pub. Tilly and Millie went to get the drinks and found out why the pub was so busy... the drinks were cheaper! Ten minutes later the two girls returned with a tray of drinks, and the group were all talking about what they were looking forward to.

"I'm looking forward to visiting the Houses of Parliament tomorrow", Melissa said.

"I'm looking forward to watching Mamma Mia", Lottie said.

"OMG! It's so romantic, I saw it a few years ago with my family", Ella said.

"Spare me the details Ella!" Oliver exclaimed.

"Oh crap! I forgot my Mum has arranged for Chris Rhunan to meet us", Olivia said.

"I think that is really nice of him, he must get lots of requests as a MP!" Melissa said.

"Quite right, but not everyone lives next door to him Mel", Oliver responded.

"We better be on our best behaviour, we don't want my mum having a go at me", Olivia added.

"He was a head teacher before he became an MP", Oliver said.

"What time are we meeting him again?" Jake asked.

"Ten-thirty and we are having a free lunch thrown into it as well", Melissa said.

"Nobody told me there will be food", Oliver responded.

"I wonder why", Melissa replied.

"Hey Olly, imagine if you had tried to get out of going thinking it will be boring and missing out on the free grub", Darcy said.

"Posh grub- it is the Houses of Parliament we are going to", Tilly responded.

"Hope it's not too posh… bite size butties would be great", Oliver added.

"Come on everyone let's go back to the hotel and have a good night sleep, we've got a lot to get through tomorrow", Sophie said.

Chapter 8

The following morning the teenagers went downstairs and they all met in reception.

"Morning all!" Aiden said.

"Let's grab a bite to eat and go straight to the Houses of Parliament", Tilly ordered.

"Is it McDonald's then?" Paige questioned.

They all headed towards McDonalds and there was a big queue to the entrance of the restaurant. Oliver found some seats upstairs. Aiden and Jake took the orders and Melissa paid for it all. Fifteen minutes later the boys came back with the food and the drinks.

They were all enjoying their food and was having a conversation about their experience in London so far. A short while later they had all finished their breakfast.

"Time to go guys", Melissa said.

Everyone headed downstairs and started walking towards the Houses of Parliament, arriving dead on ten-thirty. They walked into the building and were met by MP Chris Rhunan. He shook every single one of the teenager's hands.

"We have got so many questions for you Mr Rhunan", Millie said.

"Have we?" Jake whispered to Aiden.

"Behave guys", Melissa nudged her friends.

"Well let's hope I can answer them for you", Mr Rhunan said.

Mr Rhunan directed the teenagers to his dining hall and asked the attendants to make them each a cup of tea and a slice of cake. He was very friendly and answered all of the questions that they wanted to ask. Aiden was the future politician amongst them; the questions he was asking were mind blowing as half of the teenagers did not have a clue what he was talking about. Olivia surprised them the most by asking Mr Rhunan about the Welsh Assembly. He told Olivia he would arrange for her to meet Anne Jones, one of the Welsh Assembly Members.

"You would think he was arranging a date with Olly Murs for her, just look at her", Jake said.

"When do we get the food?" Oliver asked.

"I thought we might see the Prime Minister somewhere while we have been taken around", Darcy responded.

"A bit difficult that one Darcy, he is visiting our troops in Afghanistan on a two day visit", Aiden explained.

"Oh, don't talk about Afghanistan; I hate the thought of war", Olivia responded.

"Unfortunately it's a fact of life", Aiden replied.

"My cousin Peter is out there now and it's his second time", Millie said.

"What's his role?" Aiden asked.

"He is on medical emergency helicopters- that's all I know- and he should be home for Christmas", Millie replied.

"Oh that's nice him coming home to his family for Christmas", Melissa said.

Ben was secretly taking photographs while the teenagers were being shown around.

"Ben, you know we aren't allowed to take photographs", Ella said.

"I know, but I just thought I'd get a few to post on Facebook with us doing something intellectual", Ben replied.

"US! Intellectual", Tilly butted in.

"I wasn't including you Tilly", Ben snapped.

Mr Rhunan announced to the teenagers that lunch was ready if they could make their way to the terrace dining room.

"Follow me guys", Oliver said.

"Typical Oliver, first in the queue", Melissa joked.

They all entered the dining room, however Lottie was a bit disappointed.

"It's like our school canteen; I thought it would be really posh", Lottie said whilst sighing.

"Here's me thinking we would get a good meal, but all we have got is little butties and party food", Oliver said.

"I can feel a KFC coming on", Jake said.

"It looks like we can go after this", Paige said.

"I'm tired of all this walking we have done", Melissa said sighing.

"It's been interesting though", Ben pointed out.

"It will be three o'clock before we get back to the hotel and we have to be out again for Mamma Mia at half past five", Lottie said.

"Half past five! Cheap ticket times", Oliver responded.

Everyone thanked Mr Rhunan for a lovely time and walked out of the building. They were about to board a bus back to the hotel when Oliver realized he had left his back pack in the dining room.

"Oh you Wally", Jake said.

"Well you can head back on your own because I'm not doing that walk again", Melissa said.

"I will come with you Oliver", Aiden offered.

The two boys both ran inside in the building to get Oliver's back pack while everyone sat down in their seats on the bus waiting for them. Five minutes later the two boys came back with Oliver's back pack. They both sat down and the bus took off. The bus driver dropped the teenagers off at their hotel.

"I think I will have a lie down, I'm knackered", Melissa said whilst yawning.

"Why don't we take your wheelchair to the theatre tonight?" Sophie suggested.

"NO WAY!!" Melissa shouted in distress.

"Just listen for once!" Darcy replied angrily.

"They are right Melissa, even you are expecting a long queue and you will be grateful if you get to have a sit down if you are getting tired", Olivia added.

"And I'll have a ride back if you don't want too", Ella said whilst smiling.

"In the queue Ella", Sophie replied glaring at her friend.

"DON'T fight over who's getting a free ride in the wheelchair, you can bet Oliver will jump in the minute I get out of it", Melissa stressed.

"You got it one Mel", Darcy added.

The boys were all ready to go and they were waiting in the foyer for the girls to come down. Seconds later all the girls emerged from the lift with Sophie carrying Melissa's wheelchair.

"Is that for me?" Oliver questioned sarcastically.

"Keep your hands off; it's taken a miracle to persuade Melissa given all that walking this morning. We all told her that she should take the wheelchair because there will be a long queue for Mamma Mia", Sophie explained.

"Will you all stop making a bloody fuss and let's get going", Melissa responded as she sat down in the wheelchair.

"I will push if everyone's ok with that", Aiden said.

"Gentleman as well as a politician Mr Perry", Oliver said jokingly.

"FOR GOODNESS SAKE! Let's GO" Melissa shouted.

All the teenagers walked to the theatre with Aiden pushing Melissa in the wheelchair. It took fifteen minutes to get there. They walked into the theatre and there was, of course, a massive queue.

"What did I say? This queue has got to be a mile long", Sophie complained.

"You do exaggerate Sophie and they have at least six box offices open so we shouldn't be that long", Millie responded.

"I have got a good idea", Oliver said.

Oliver walked over to the entrance of the auditorium and spoke to the security man about Melissa being in a wheelchair, requesting if they could go to the front of the queue and get in first.

"Where is he going?" Jake questioned.

"How do we know?" Aiden responded.

Five minutes later Oliver came back from talking to the security guard.

"Come on guys follow me", Oliver ordered.

"What are you talking about?" Lottie questioned.

"Well I told the security guard that our friend is disabled and we need to get her in first because she is getting stressed that she has to wait in this queue", Oliver explained.

"STRESSING! Now I'm stressing, what did he say?" Melissa responded angrily.

"We can go to the front of the queue… I reckon that's one of my best moves today", Oliver replied.

All the teenagers walked to the front of the queue and when they got there the security guard looked at Melissa in a serious way.

"You don't look disabled young lady" the security guard questioned.

"Can I ask what disabled looks like?" Melissa said sarcastically,

"That's not a very nice thing to say", Lottie responded.

"Show him your left arm Mel", Paige said.

"Show him your right arm more like", Lottie responded,

"Sorry I didn't mean it to sound like that, we get so many people pulling all sorts of tricks to jump the queue and then those who patiently wait get annoyed", the security guard explained.

"Making your life difficult hey mate", Oliver responded.

"I'm sorry for being harsh young lady, you can go through enjoy the show", the security guard said.

"Thank you very much", Melissa replied whilst shaking the guard's hand.

All the teenagers walked into the auditorium and were confronted with nothing but stairs.

"Now how are we going to get Mel down the stairs without her getting out of the wheelchair?" Jake questioned.

"Two of us could lift Mel in our arms, and one of us could hold the wheelchair", Oliver suggested.

"That's a good idea", Lottie agreed.

"I'M NOT A BABY!" Melissa said angrily.

"It's the only way we can do this", Ella said.

"I'm not helpless guys, I can get out of my wheelchair and walk down the stairs, I've done it before so many times", Melissa said firmly.

"Are you sure?" Aiden asked.

"Yes, give me your arm!" Melissa said linking Aiden's arm down the stairs.

Ben carried the wheelchair and the rest of the gang followed Aiden and Melissa to the front row. They all sat in their assigned seats. Melissa sat at the end of the row by Aiden in her wheelchair.

"I will go and get some refreshments from the kiosk", Oliver said whilst walking up the stairs.

"Are you sharing this time?" Aiden questioned.

"No chance, you can get your own", Oliver responded.

"Well I will go and get the programs and some more refreshments that we can all share", Jake said looking at Oliver.

The two boys returned a few minutes later as the show was just starting. The first half was very elegant and exciting to watch. The curtains closed for the interval and the lights came on.

"Ice cream time guys", Oliver stated.

"Here, I will give you the money to pay for the ice creams", Melissa said handing the money to Oliver.

"Thanks Mel", Oliver replied.

"I will come and help you", Aiden said whilst walking up the stairs.

The two boys returned seconds later with twelve ice cream tubes. Fifteen minutes later the lights went down for the second half.

The second half was longer than the first half, and it was an amazing performance. Everyone was up on their feet dancing to the most successful songs in the world of Abba.

At the end of the performance, Aiden linked Melissa's arm as they walked up the stairs and Oliver carried her wheelchair followed by everyone else. They all emerged from the building and saw a taxi across the road; they walked across the road and helped Melissa into the taxi. On the way to the hotel the teenagers could not stop talking about the show.

"So guys what did you think of the show?" Melissa asked her friends.

"I thought it was very exciting to watch, the music, the atmosphere, it was an outstanding performance", Darcy commented.

"I thought it was romantic at times", Ella commented.

"You would", Lottie said.

"Shut up Lottie!" Ella responded.

Everyone went silent for a few minutes, then Paige spoke.

"What are we doing tomorrow?" Paige questioned.

"We are going on the London Eye tomorrow morning, then seeing as it's our last night we can just have a chill before we go out", Aiden replied.

"Sounds good to me", Jake said.

They arrived back at the hotel and Aiden paid the taxi driver. They all jumped out f the taxi with Melissa's wheelchair.

"Do you guys fancy a quick drink before we go up to our rooms?" Oliver questioned.

"No I'm done in Oliver, I'm going to bed", Aiden replied.

"Aiden's right we all need an early night to get up for the London

Eye tomorrow", Melissa agreed.

"Good night guys", Jake said.

The girls went in the lift with Melissa in her wheelchair and the boys took the stairs up to their rooms.

Chapter 9

The next morning the teenagers all got dressed and brushed their teeth ready to go downstairs for breakfast. They all went into the dining room and sat at a large table in the middle of the hall. The breakfast menu was a help yourself buffet, and one by one the teenagers got their breakfast and drinks and all tucked in.

"I'm so excited for the London Eye", Ella commented.

"Me too, I love going on big rides like a rollercoaster", Darcy commented.

"I don't like rides at all, they make me feel sick", Melissa disagreed.

"If you feel like that then don't go on it", Lottie responded.

"No, I want to, I don't want to miss out on all the exciting buildings and features to look from a high view", Melissa replied.

"To make you feel better one of the lads will come sit with you and hold your hand", Millie said.

"WE WILL!!" The three boys all said in unison.

After finishing their breakfast the teenagers headed towards the exit of the hotel.

"Do you want the wheelchair Melissa?" Olivia questioned.

"No, I will be ok for today, I don't need to be in it all the time", Melissa replied.

"Ok it's your choice", Olivia responded.

The teenagers all started walking along the River Thames to get to the London Eye. It took them twenty five minutes to get there. When they arrived they got out their phones and took selfies and photographs of each other with the London Eye and the River Thames behind them.

"Wow! I didn't realize how big this ride is", Paige stated.

"I love these types of rides, so it doesn't scare me", Darcy said whilst smirking at Melissa.

"Look at that queue it must be the most popular tourist attraction", Sophie said.

"Did you know that The London Eye took seven years to construct and was designed by number of architects including Mark Sparrowhawk, David Marks and Julia Barfield?" Ben stated.

Everyone except Ella just looked at him with a glare.

"Please, this isn't a history lesson", Oliver responded.

"What? I was just giving a fact about The London Eye, what's wrong with that?" Ben responded back.

"It's just that you always think you know it all and it's getting on our nerves", Aiden replied angrily.

"Come on guys let's not argue", Paige said calmly.

"Yeah the queue's moving now", Ella added.

"We need to divide into partners to go on the wheel", Brooke stated.

"I'm going with Melissa!" Aiden, Jake, and Oliver said in unison.

"Guys will you please stop this fighting over me, it's getting ridiculous, Aiden can keep me company and you two can go behind us if you want?" Melissa responded.

"Ok, we will be your other bodyguards", Oliver joked.

Once they partnered up in the queue, they each received a ticket from the security guards and boarded the wheel. They strapped themselves and the wheel started to go up.

Melissa hung onto the rail for dear life, Aiden saw this and put his arm around her shoulder.

"It's ok Mel, I'm here for you. How are you feeling?" Aiden asked gently touching her shoulder.

"I feel like I'm going to be sick", Melissa replied.

"Well just don't down or side to side and focus on the horizon as they always say. I will be right here if you need a hand to hold", Aiden said gently.

"Thanks Aiden, you are too kind", Melissa replied as she gave him a quick kiss on the cheek.

Some time later, Melissa was still feeling sick and was shaking like a leaf. She looked at Aiden and grabbed his hand and started crying.

"Still feeling sick Mel?" Aiden questioned.

"Yeah I can't cope, it makes your tummy go funny", Melissa replied in distress.

"You're shaking like a leaf! Come here". Aiden pulled Melissa into a hug.

"Is everything alright up there Aiden?" Jake yelled up to the upper carriage

"Not really Jake, Mel is still feeling sick and she's shaking like a leaf", Aiden replied.

"Is there anything we can do to help?" Oliver asked.

"You can help her think about good things that we have done in London that will make her keep her mind off this bloody ride!!" Aiden responded.

"Right, ok Mel…"

"Yeah", Melissa replied.

"Think about the good things that we have done in London so far, and just relax", Oliver said.

"Ok I will try", Melissa replied.

Melissa was thinking about when they went to Madame Tussauds and they all went in the dungeons. She held Aiden's hand. Melissa knew that she had feeling for him, but she didn't realize how much she loved him. It was going well for Melissa keeping her mind occupied when all of a sudden Ben came out with all of these facts about The London Eye and that set her off again.

"Did you know that The London Eye was often called the Millennium Wheel when it was first opened? As well as that The London Eye is not the first big wheel to…"

"BEN WILL YOU SHUT UP AND STOP TALKING ABOUT YOUR STUPID FACTS ABOUT THE LONDON EYE AND STOP SAYING THE WORD WHEEL IT'S MAKING ME FEEL SICK!!" Melissa shouted from the rooftops.

"Alright Mel, calm down", Ben responded.

"There is no need to shout like that", Ella added.

"Oh shut up both of you, it's not Mel's fault that she's frightened of the height of the ride, don't speak to her like that", Aiden responded.

Melissa couldn't believe what she just heard. Aiden stuck up for her and she loved that way about him he was so kind and caring. She couldn't help herself but kiss Aiden passionately on the lips. She quickly pulled away feeling embarrassed.

"What was that for?" Aiden questioned.

"To say thank you", Melissa replied.

"There is more to it than that, I know you", Aiden teased.

Melissa took a deep breath and put her hands in Aiden's.

"Aiden, I've been waiting a long time to say this and I feel now this could be a good time to say...

"I love you!" They both said at the same time.

"Really?" You feel the same way as I do", Melissa questioned.

"Of course I do. I've loved you since you became my best friend", Aiden replied.

"I don't what to say to that, I'm speechless",

"Will you be my girlfriend Mel?" Aiden questioned.

"Of course I will". Melissa and Aiden held each other close and kissed passionately.

Ten minutes Aiden and Melissa finished their kissing session, and they were all loved up. Aiden put his arm around Melissa's neck and Melissa rested her head on Aiden's neck.

Jake and Oliver were watching from above and they were pleased that Aiden and Melissa had finally got together.

"Mel's not as scared as she was before", Oliver said.

"Yeah I know, I knew that they would get together at some point", Jake added.

The ride soon stopped for departing, Aiden helped Melissa get off the ride and they walked to their mates holding hands. All the friends turned around to see Melissa and Aiden holding hands. Some faces lit up with excitement, and some wanted to know the details about what they saw.

"Why are you guys holding hands?" Darcy questioned.

"Is this what I think it is?" Brooke added.

Aiden and Melissa just kept smiling at each other.

"We are waiting!" Paige said jokingly.

"We are now and officially a couple!" Melissa exclaimed.

Everyone congratulated the happy couple with hugs from the girls and hi fives from the boys.

"I'm so glad that you two are together", Ben said.

"Thanks Ben, and I'm sorry for shouting at you like that before I was just frightened of the ride that's all", Melissa apologized giving her friend a hug.

"No worries Mel", Ben responded.

"So what happened on the ride that made you guys become boyfriend and girlfriend?" Millie questioned.

"We kissed for ten minutes and admitted our feelings to each other", Aiden replied.

"More like an hour!" Oliver said sarcastically.

"Let's go back to the hotel and freshen up for tonight's celebration", Sophie said cheerfully.

It took all the teenagers twenty-five minutes to walk back to the hotel. They walked into reception and went upstairs to their rooms to freshen up.

.

Chapter 10

A few hours later, the teenagers all started getting ready to go out. The girls were all in one room. Melissa, Ella and Millie were all putting their make-up and getting dressed whilst having a chat, the rest of the girls were getting showers.

"I'm really happy that you and Aiden are together at last", Millie commented.

"Thanks Mill, I just felt that this was my moment to express my feelings towards him", Melissa replied.

"I'm also really happy that you and Aiden are together", Ella commented.

Melissa turned around to face Ella who was crying as she said it. She went over to her friend and gave her a hug.

"Ella, I'm sorry I shouted at you and Ben on the ride, I was just so scared of the height", Melissa apologized.

"It's ok Mel, don't worry about it", Ella replied.

Some of the girls came out of the bathroom and got dressed into their party clothes.

"So… what do you want to do tonight girls?" Olivia questioned.

"Well since it's our last night here, I think we should see a West End show what we've not seen yet. How does that sound?" Melissa suggested.

"Yeah and we can go to Mr Wong's again for something to eat before it", Darcy replied.

"I will text Aiden to tell him what the plan is", Melissa said whilst getting her phone.

In the next room Aiden and Ben were taking their showers whilst Jake and Oliver were getting dressed. Jake was walking to the dressing table to get his hair gel when Aiden's phone buzzed. Jake looked at it and saw that Melissa had texted him, he smirked and turned to Oliver.

"Hey Ollie, look at this. Mel has just texted Aiden and has put five kisses. She must be so in love with him", Jake said.

"I know how sweet". All of a sudden Oliver had a smirk on his face.

"Hey Jake watch this..."

"What are you doing?"

"I love whining Aiden up about Melissa".

"Me too".

Oliver and Jack both walked into the bathroom when the boys were still having their showers.

"What are you guys doing in here?" Aiden responded whilst pulling the shower curtain.

"Yeah a bit of privacy will do", Ben added whilst putting his towel over himself.

"Alright calm down, we were just coming in to give you your phone because you had a text off Melissa but...

"Wait, did you just say that Mel has texted me?"

"Yeah, we thought that you might smile when we said her name", Jake said.

"Why didn't you say that in the first place instead of just barging in?"

"You were having a go at us..."

"Give me that", Aiden said snatching the phone off Oliver.

"What has your beloved Melissa texted you?" Ben said.

"She's texted what we are doing tonight, it sounds brilliant", Aiden replied.

"Did she put any kisses?" Jake questioned.

"Yes, she put five kisses- she's so sweet", Aiden replied.

"You're so in love with her, aren't you?" Oliver questioned.

"Yeah I am", Aiden responded.

"Are you going to send a flirty text to her?" Ben questioned.

"Don't know, let's wait and see", Aiden replied.

Aiden texted Melissa back and her face lit up.

"Is that Aiden by any chance?" Ella questioned her best friend with a smirk.

"Yeah it is actually", Melissa responded whilst smiling.

"What has he put Mel?" Darcy questioned.

"He said that the plan for tonight sounds brilliant", Melissa said going bright red.

"Why have you gone bright red?" Olivia questioned.

"Yeah let's see what else he's put", Sophie added.

"NO! Mind your own business", Melissa responded.

"Aww come on Mel!" Brooke whined.

"NO! It's personal and embarrassing", Melissa responded angrily.

"Oh ok". Ella said and quickly turned around to grab Melissa's phone.

"Hey give it back"

Ella read the text out loud to the girls and teased Melissa.

"The plan sounds brilliant Mel, can't wait to celebrate our relationship as a couple... love you loads!!"Aww that is so cute Mel", Ella said whilst the girls were laughing. Melissa gave Ella a dirty look and grabbed her phone.

"We are really sorry Mel, we shouldn't have laughed", Millie said seriously.

"Yeah, I shouldn't have read the text out loud", Ella added.

"Just forget it now girls, let's go and have a nice night out", Melissa responded calmly.

Melissa and the girls went out the door at the same time Aiden and the boys came out of their room. The teenagers all stared at each other in confusion and it was all a bit awkward, until Jake spoke.

"How come you girls came out at the same time as us?"

"We thought that we would get dressed early, what's your excuse?" Olivia questioned.

"We thought we would do the same thing", Oliver replied suspiciously.

"Anyway, you girls look gorgeous", Ben commented.

Melissa, Ella and Darcy linked their boyfriend's arms whilst the rest of the teenagers walked ahead of them. They reached reception and Oliver went to order a taxi when Lottie pointed out they should do more exercise. They all exited the hotel and started walking to Mr. Wong's Restaurant.

Chapter 11

They all went inside and sat at the front of the restaurant by the window. Mr Wong came over to the table with menus, a notebook and pen.

"Welcome back guys, it's nice to see you again".

"Nice to see you again Mr Wong", Darcy said.

"Do you know what you want to order?"

"Yes, can we have a bottle of prosecco and a big banquet for all of us to share", Aiden said.

"Coming right up".

Moments later Mr Wong came over with a bottle of prosecco and a bowl of prawn crackers to start. Jake popped open the prosecco and it exploded everywhere. They all quickly put their glasses near the bottle so Jake could pour the drink. Aiden tapped his glass and stood up.

"I would like to make a toast".

"Oh no here we go", Oliver moaned.

"It won't take long, I just want to say I'm really happy that Melissa and I are finally together, I've been waiting for this for a long time and I've finally got my girl!"

"To Aiden and Melissa!" Jake said raising his glass.

Everyone raised their glasses. Melissa had a tear in her eye and Aiden kisses her on the cheek. Everyone was having a really good chat about the recent events that have happened during their time in London and Oliver had eaten all of the prawn crackers and was moaning about the wait for the food.

"How long does it take to do a banquet, I'm starving".

"Starving! You can't be starving you just ate all the prawn crackers!" Ben responded angrily.

"I know but I'm still hungry".

"Let's have a selfie of all of us at the table having a good time", Millie said as she got her phone.

Millie took a selfie on her phone and she sent it to everyone on whatsapp. Ten minutes later, Mr Wong bought a massive banquet over to the table with loads of different foods to share.

"About time!" Oliver exclaimed.

He quickly dived in and grabbed every dish of food that was in the banquet, leaving everyone sharing out equally. They all tucked in very quickly and enjoyed their meal.

An hour later some of the teenagers felt a bit tipsy and some felt as if they had a bit too much prosecco.

"I think it's time we ordered another bottle of prosecco, don't you?" Sophie exclaimed.

"I don't bloody think so; we've got a show we need to go to!" Melissa said firmly.

"We don't want to turn up to the theatre drunk", Darcy added.

"I feel sick, I think I've had too much prosecco", Tilly stated.

"It looks like you are, judging by your face", Oliver joked.

"I will get the bill", Jake said as he stood up.

"No, sit down Jake, I will shout over to Mr Wong", Sophie responded.

Sophie stood on the table and shouted over to the waiter.

"EXCUSE ME MR WONG CAN WE HAVE THE BILL PLEASE!!"

All the people in the restaurant turned around to look at Sophie with strange faces. Mr Wong just nodded his head in embarrassment.

"Sit down Sophie; you are embarrassing yourself and us!" Melissa responded.

"You must be drunk", Olivia added.

"I'm not drunk at all, I was just trying to get his attention to come over to us", Sophie responded.

"Well you didn't need to stand on the table and shout like that!" Aiden argued.

"Oh whatever!" Sophie said in a huff.

Mr Wong returned and placed the bill on the table with some sweets.

"Pay when you are ready!"

They were all deciding who was going to pay. Oliver was complaining about the sweets.

"I will pay guys since it's a celebration for Aiden and I".

"No, you have paid for everything else Mel, it's our turn to do something nice for return in favour", Jake offered.

"Aww thanks Jake, that's very kind of you", Melissa replied.

Jake went to the bar to pay for the meal and prosecco whilst everyone else was getting ready to go.

"That sweet was rubbish", Oliver complained.

"What was wrong with it?" Paige asked.

"It was too small; it had no flavour to it".

"What did you expect Oliver, a big lemon bar or something?" Paige said sarcastically.

"No, I just thought it would be bigger that's all".

Chapter 12

Jake returned from the bar, and everyone walked outside the door and said thank you to the waiters. They all linked arms and walked to the theatre.

"Ok guys- here is where we are sitting", Melissa said handing out the tickets.

They walked upstairs to the auditorium to watch Wicked. Ben and Ella went to get the programs, Brooke and Olivia went to get the refreshments, and the rest of the group passed their tickets to the security guards to enter to enter the theatre. They all sat in the upper centre and Ben gave everyone a program to read and the girls opened a bag of sweets.

"These sweets are to share with you guys not like Oliver who just buys his own!!" Brooke said glaring at Oliver whilst passing the sweets around.

Lottie got out her phone and took selfies and photos whilst they were waiting for the show Wicked to begin. Seconds later the lights went down. The music kicked in. And the curtains went up for the first half of the performance. People were clapping and cheering as the first scene started. One superfast hour later, the curtain fell. The lights went up for the interval and the dash for ice creams began.

"Thank god there is Ice cream in the interval; I need to get rid of the taste from that AWFUL sweet!!" Oliver said.

Oliver and Aiden went to get the ice creams. Some of the girls went to the toilet to freshen up. Soon after everyone had come back from the toilet and with the ice creams it was time for the second half of the performance. The lights went down. And the curtain went up for the start of the second half.

Half an hour later the show come to an end. Everyone was walking out of the theatre slowly in an orderly fashion.

"It's only half eight, what do you guys want to do now?" Jake asked his friends.

"I was thinking about going to an Ice Bar", Melissa replied.

"What's an Ice Bar?" Aiden questioned.

"I'll look it up on Google", Ben said as he got out his phone and searched for it. "It says here that an Ice Bar is basically just an ice hotel with ice sculptors and things like that".

"I want to go", Sophie said excitedly.

"Me too, it will be a good laugh", Oliver added.

"How long is it to get there?" Darcy questioned.

"Why? Are you tired", Oliver questioned.

"No, I just want to know how far it is", Darcy replied.

"According to Google it takes eights to get there from the theatre", Ben said.

"Let's go then", Aiden said.

Chapter 13

Everyone started walking to the Ice Bar. When they got there they went in the porch to take their coats off and put on some waterproof suits, waterproof shoes, and a thermal hat to put on for an extra layer of warmth.

"There is no way I'm wearing these!" Millie complained.

"They are only for extra warmth Millie", Darcy stated.

"It will spoil my look", Millie responded.

"Oh stop being such a drama queen Millie, just put them on", Melissa said angrily.

They all went inside the Ice Bar and their first impressions were positive.

"This looks incredible", Brooke commented.

"I agree, the sculptors look amazing", Ella agreed.

"Bloody hell! It's like an arctic in here, even with the suits on", Oliver said shivering.

A waiter came over to the teenagers and gave them each a leaflet about the Ice Bar and the menu for the drinks.

"What do you guys fancy to drink?" Aiden questioned.

"I quite fancy a cocktail". Melissa said.

"They are very expensive though", Jake pointed out.

Everyone ordered what they wanted to drink and whilst they were waiting, Oliver was touching the sculptors and Millie and

Darcy were taking photographs of themselves and the sculptors.

"Oliver, you aren't allowed to touch the sculptures", Melissa said sharply.

"I know that Mel, I just like to feel the cold ice".

"Mel, take some photos of me and Darcy by the ice sculptures", Millie ordered whilst handing the phone to her friend.

"I thought you didn't want people to see your thermal suits".

"Yeah well I've changed my mind", Millie responded.

Millie and Darcy were doing their best poses for the camera. The waiter came over to the table with the drinks that the teenagers had ordered. Everyone was enjoying their drinks and they also tried each other's to taste and try all the different flavours.

"Why don't we have professional photographs to take home as a souvenir", Millie suggested.

"Yeah that would be cool", Melissa replied.

They all went up to the professional photographer; they posed for the camera and were each issued a copy of their photo to take home. After a while the teenagers were all getting tired and decided to head back to the hotel. They jumped a taxi back to their hotel and went straight upstairs to their rooms.

Chapter 14

The next morning the teenagers were up bright and early. The girls were putting their stuff away in their suitcases and the boys were having their showers.

"I can't believe we are going today", Melissa said with a sigh.

"I know, the time has just flown by", Darcy responded.

"We've done loads of exciting things whilst we've been here", Ella said cheerfully.

"Yeah really good memories", Sophie added.

"I wish we could stay a bit longer", Olivia said with a sad face.

After the boys had their showers and the girls had packed their suitcases they all went downstairs ready to have their breakfast. They all put their luggage in reception and headed towards the dining room. They decided to sit in the middle of the restaurant on a large table. The waitress came over to the table and asked what they wanted to drink. Breakfast was an all you could eat buffet.

Chapter 15

An hour later the teenagers had all finished their breakfast and were deciding what to do before they headed back home.

"What time do we need to be at the train station for?" Ella questioned.

"Well I've booked a taxi at twelve o'clock to take us to the train station. We board at quarter to one", Ben said.

"How about we go shopping around London for a bit and..."

"I'm not going shopping with you girls, you take hours just in ne shop", Oliver moaned.

"Just hear me out Olly, we can go shopping and have a drink and a sit down in a café before we go to the train station", Olivia explained.

"That sounds good, we haven't been shopping yet and it will be nice to look around", Tilly agreed.

"Ok then, but don't expect me and the boys to hold your shopping bags for you", Oliver responded.

Jake went over to the receptionist to ask whether they could collect their luggage after they had completed some shopping. They all headed out of the hotel and walked to the Shopping Centre. They went inside the Westfield London Shopping Centre and Melissa was shaking like a leaf as she saw there were escalators.

"Why are you shaking Mel?" Darcy asked putting her arm around her friend's shoulder.

"There are loads of escalators, I'm terrified of them", Melissa replied.

"I will hold your hand", Aiden offered.

"Or we can use the lift", Sophie suggested.

"I think it's best if I hold your hand Aiden, it will be more comfortable for me", Melissa said as she grabbed her boyfriend's hand.

They all walked on the escalator and headed to the shops on the first floor. Melissa felt a lot better with the help of her boyfriend.

"Are you ok now Mel?" Aiden asked his girlfriend.

"Yeah I'm ok now, thanks Aiden I feel more comfortable with you beside me", Melissa replied as she gave Aiden a kiss on the cheek.

"What shops do you guys want to go in?" Millie asked her friends.

"Well the boys and I need some more Sport clothes for P.E in college, so we are going to Sports Direct", Ben said.

"Ok then, the girls and I will go to New Look to have some look at some clothes", Ella said.

"Meet by Harrods at eleven o'clock, we will have a look around and a drink and walk back to the hotel ready for the taxi", Paige ordered.

"Ok, see you in an hour girls", Oliver said.

They all separated into two groups and went shopping. In Sports Direct the boys were looking for sports T-shirts, and shorts for their Football Tournament in P.E. They were trying things on with sexy poses and finally decided to get a blue and yellow sports kit. They all paid for their things and went to go and buy some trainers from JD. Meanwhile in New Look, the girls were trying on different styles of dresses in front of the mirror.

"What do you think of this sparkly dress girls?" Ella asked her friends.

"It looks amazing on you Ella", Darcy commented.

"Does my stomach look fat in this top?" Lottie questioned.

"Don't be stupid Lottie, you look gorgeous", Tilly commented.

Melissa came out of the fitting room with a purple dress and white converse.

"Wit Whoo Mel!" Brooke commented.

"Aiden will love it", Paige added.

"Thanks girls, I thought it would look perfect for the summer disco in college", Melissa said excitedly.

"Have you decided what clothes you want guys?" Millie asked.

"Yes all sorted lets go pay for ou things", Melissa replied.

The girls went over to the till and payed for their items.

"Should we walk to Harrods and have a look around there?" Olivia suggested.

"Yeah ok, I will just ring Aiden to say what we are doing, you guys can still have another look around if you want", Melissa exclaimed.

Melissa went outside the shop to call her boyfriend. In JD Sports the boys were trying on different styles of trainers when Aiden's phone was vibrating in his trousers.

"Oooh... someone's pants are vibrating!" Jake joked.

Aiden jumped out of his skin and quickly got his phone out of his pocket. His face lit up when he saw the caller ID, however he didn't notice that the boys were looking at him with smirks.

"Is that Melissa by any chance?" Ben questioned.

"Mind your own business! I'm going outside", Aiden responded.

Aiden went outside the shop to answer the phone call.

"Hi Mel, what's up?" Aiden exclaimed.

"The girls and I have finished in New Look and are going to walk to Harrods now", Melissa explained.

"Ok babe, me and the boys are finished in JD now anyway, so we will meet you in Harrods in a minute".

"Looking forward to seeing you!"

"You too!"

"Love you Aiden!" Melissa flirted.

"Love you too Mel!" Aiden flirted back.

The two love birds both hung up and went inside the shop to their friends.

"Ok girls let's go!" Melissa ordered.

The girls walked to Harrods linking arms. The automatic doors slide open and as they walked in the shop was immaculate.

"Wow this looks absolutely amazing", Ella commented.

"Everywhere is so shiny and immaculate", Lottie added.

Melissa and the girls decided to look at different things to buy as souvenirs and gifts for their family. Aiden and the boys walked in the shop with their sports bags and were amazed by the spotlessness of the floors and how huge the shop was.

"Bloody hell! This shop is huge compared to the other shops in London", Oliver stated.

"How are we going to find the girls?" Jake questioned.

"I will text Mel to see where they are", Aiden said as he got out his phone.

Melissa received Aiden's text and she texted back to say that she was in the merchandise section with the girls. Aiden told the boys to follow him to where the girls were. The girls were looking for souvenir handbags whilst Melissa was looking at the merchandise notebooks and stationary sets for her writing.

Aiden and the boys were walking down the aisle and Aiden put his arms around Melissa's waist.

"Hi beautiful!"

Melissa turned around and kissed her boyfriend on the lips. All the girls said "Aww" in unison. The two love birds quickly pulled away from each other feeling embarrassed.

"So, what are you girls buying? Anything special?" Jake asked.

"We are just getting some souvenirs for family and ourselves", Darcy replied.

"I'm going to buy this sparkly notebook to write my stories", Melissa said.

"That's great because you write the most amazing stories!" Aiden commented.

"Aww thank you", Melissa replied gently touching Aiden's arm.

The teenagers were looking around the store to buy some more things, when Jake came across a Black Staffie dog handbag.

"Hey Aiden, look what I found?" Jake said.

"What is it?" Aiden questioned.

"Mel loves dogs, so I thought you could get her this black Staffie handbag", Jake suggested whilst showing Aiden the item.

"Isn't it a bit babyish?" Aiden questioned.

"If you buy this for her she will love you even more", Jake pointed out.

"Black Staffie handbag, you are coming with me", Aiden said in a cocky voice.

Aiden went to the till to pay, whilst Jake and the gang were still looking around.

Chapter 16

Once everyone had decided what they wanted to buy, they all went to the tills to pay. They decided to take hot drinks out with them because of how much they spent in Harrods; they didn't have a lot of time to sit down. They headed towards the taxi rank. Aiden told the taxi driver if they could go back to the hotel to get their luggage and drop them off at the train station.

They all got out of the taxi and quickly grabbed their suitcases from the storage cupboard and went straight back in the taxi. They arrived at the train station in plenty of time. They sat in the café drinking their hot drinks they took out and was showing each other their gifts that they bought, but a very particular person wanted to show his girlfriend he special gift that he had bought her.

"Mel, I've got you something special from Harrods", Aiden said giving the shopping bag to Melissa.

"Is it an engagement ring?" Ben asked sarcastically.

"SHUT UP BEN AND KEEP YOUR COMMENTS TO YOURSELF!!!"

Melissa reached inside the bag to find her special gift, and her face said it all.

"Aww Aiden that is so cute I love, thank you so much", Melissa said giving her boyfriend a hug.

"Your welcome Mel", Aiden replied with a smile on his face.

"Creep!" Oliver said sarcastically.

"Excuse me I'm not a creep, I've bought a gift for my girlfriend because I love her, and I want her to be happy" Aiden replied.

"Aww!!" All the girls said in unison whilst Melissa went bright red.

"Can someone get me a bucket because I'm going to be sick", Oliver said in a sarcastic tone.

"How we put up with you on this trip, I don't know", Jake said jokingly.

"I can say the same thing about you mate", Oliver responded back.

"It looks like the train's here guys", Sophie said.

The teenagers grabbed their suitcases and shopping bags and started walking to the boarding gates. They all got their boarding tickets out ready to give to the assistance. After boarding the train, Aiden and Jake put all the girl's suitcases and their own suitcases on the trays above their heads. They were all talking about what a wonderful time they have had in London all the way home.

Printed in Great Britain
by Amazon